Why does there have to be so much Kissing?

It goes on
everywhere,

No More Kissing!

EMMA CHICHESTER CLARK

An imprint of HarperCollins*Publishers*

for Rodney

Have you read these picture books by Emma Chichester Clark?

More!
Follow My Leader!
I Love You, Blue Kangaroo!
Where Are You, Blue Kangaroo!
It Was You, Blue Kangaroo!

First published in hardback in Great Britain by Andersen Press Ltd in 2001
First published in paperback by Collins Picture Books in 2002

1 3 5 7 9 10 8 6 4 2
ISBN: 0-00-713105-4

Collins Picture Books is an imprint of the Children's Division, part of HarperCollins Publishers Ltd.

A CIP catalogue record for this title is available from the British Library.

The HarperCollins website address is: www.fireandwater.com
Printed and bound in Hong Kong

all over the place,
especially mummies kissing babies.

I wish no one had invented kissing.

And I wish no one
would kiss ME,

especially...

people
I don't KNOW!

My family do it too,
all the time.

They kiss Hello,
then they kiss Goodbye.

They kiss Good Morning.

they kiss Good Night.

When my cousin, Mimi, hurt her finger, everyone had to kiss it better. She loves kissing. She'll kiss anything...

... but not ME!
My mum is always telling us to kiss and make up.

I've told all my family – my mum, my dad, my grandma, all my cousins, my uncle and my aunts…

No more kissing!

But it makes

no difference

at all !

I'm glad I'm not
a baby any more.

They get more kisses
than anyone.

It doesn't matter whose
baby they are, or how much
they squeak or squeal...

...or screech,
everyone wants to
kiss them. So I knew
what was going
to happen ...

... when our new baby came.
He screamed his head off.

The more they kissed him,
the more he screamed.
The more he screamed,
the more they kissed him.

"STOP!" I shouted.
STOP!

"Can't you see he doesn't like it?"

"Perhaps *you'd* like to hold him?" asked my grandma.

First, I showed him my aeroplane,
but he just cried.

Next, I made funny faces,
but he cried even more.
Then, I juggled some bananas.

He cried and cried and cried.
Now what shall I do? I wondered.
"What's the matter, little brother?"
His eyes popped open.
We looked at each other, eye to eye.

"Little brother," I said, and he smiled.
And then a weird thing happened,
by mistake I think. I kissed him.

It was lucky no one was looking.